Acting Edition

At The Wedding

by Bryna Turner

‖SAMUEL FRENCH‖

FOR PRODUCTION INQUIRIES

UNITED STATES AND CANADA
info@concordtheatricals.com
1-866-979-0447

UNITED KINGDOM AND EUROPE
licensing@concordtheatricals.co.uk
020-7054-7298

Each title is subject to availability from Concord Theatricals Corp.,
depending upon country of performance. Please be aware that *AT
THE WEDDING* may not be licensed by Concord Theatricals Corp. in
your territory. Professional and amateur producers should contact the
nearest Concord Theatricals Corp. office or licensing partner to verify
availability.

No one shall make any changes in this title(s) for the purpose of production. No part of this book may be reproduced, stored in a retrieval system, scanned, uploaded, or transmitted in any form, by any means, now known or yet to be invented, including mechanical, electronic, digital, photocopying, recording, videotaping, or otherwise, without the prior written permission of the publisher. No one shall share this title(s), or any part of this title(s), through any social media or file hosting websites.

For all inquiries regarding motion picture, television, online/digital and other media rights, please contact Concord Theatricals Corp.

MUSIC AND THIRD-PARTY MATERIALS USE NOTE

Licensees are solely responsible for obtaining formal written permission from copyright owners to use copyrighted music and/or other copyrighted third-party materials (e.g., artworks, logos) in the performance of this play and are strongly cautioned to do so. If no such permission is obtained by the licensee, then the licensee must use only original music and materials that the licensee owns and controls. Licensees are solely responsible and liable for clearances of all third-party copyrighted materials, including without limitation music, and shall indemnify the copyright owners of the play(s) and their licensing agent, Concord Theatricals Corp., against any costs, expenses, losses and liabilities arising from the use of such copyrighted third-party materials by licensees. For music, please contact the appropriate music licensing authority in your territory for the rights to any incidental music.

IMPORTANT BILLING AND CREDIT REQUIREMENTS

If you have obtained performance rights to this title, please refer to your licensing agreement for important billing and credit requirements.

AT THE WEDDING was developed, in part, by TheatreSquared as part of the Arkansas New Play Festival and premiered at Lincoln Center Theater in New York City in 2022. The production was directed by Jenna Worsham, with set design by Maruti Evans, costume design by Oana Botez, lighting design by Oona Curley, original music and sound by Fan Zhang, and stage management by Katie Kennedy. The cast was as follows:

CARLO	Mary Wiseman
CARLY	Keren Lugo
ELI	Will Rogers
MARIA	Carolyn McCormick
LEIGH	Han Van Sciver
EVA	Rebecca S'manga Frank
VICTOR	Jorge Donoso

CHARACTERS

CARLO – a wedding guest (she/her)

CARLY – a bridesmaid (she/her)

ELI – a wedding guest (he/him)

MARIA – mother of the bride (she/her)

LEIGH – a wedding guest (they/them)

EVA – the bride (she/her)

VICTOR – the cater-waiter for the evening (he/him)

SETTING

A wedding in Northern California.

TIME

Now.

NOTES ON THE PRODUCTION

All of these scenes take place on the outskirts of the big event. The more real the offstage wedding feels, the more we will understand that Carlo is avoiding it. Consider using the transitions between scenes to remind us that the wedding is still very much going on, even if it isn't our focus.

The audience members are the other guests at the wedding. The more Carlo connects with them, the more it will feel like they've fallen in with a particularly funny but ill-behaved person at a party.

Carlo is our guide, our confidant, and our fish-eye lens.

It's a comedy.

And a thousand thousand slimy things
Lived on; and so did I.

—Samuel Colerige,
The Rime of the Ancient Mariner

for the kids

1.

(At the kids' table.)

CARLO. I need to tell you something
nobody ever really thinks to tell you
until it's too late.

Too late for me, anyway.

One day you're going to fall in love

and maybe you already knew that
maybe you think you've already fallen in love

but – kids, eyes on me –

when you actually fall in love
it will feel like you are somehow suddenly
seeing the world in three dimensions for the very first
time

food will taste better
music will sound better
you will suddenly comprehend
every line in every book you've ever read
as it was meant to be comprehended

and you will marvel that you ever thought
life was worth living
before that moment
before that grace
took you and wrapped you
in its embrace

but then, kids,
and this is the part they don't tell you

one day
that love will break your heart

I know you think it won't
inevitably you convince yourself
that you are the one exception to the rule—
you must!
if you didn't believe that
you would never allow yourself to
fall so deeply into such a heaven
because you'd already be anticipating
the sting
of being cast out

but you will.

you'll fall in
and eventually
you will be cast out

I can't say that I know why
I can give you a laundry list of reasons
but none of them make any sense to me
so I won't bother wasting my breath

I can say
the fall from heaven
is the worst pain you'll feel in your life

you've felt agony before

I'm sure you have

but this
this is a sort of pain you were incapable of feeling
because it is only possible once you've truly understood
it's opposite

for the first time

for the first time in your life
that dull ache

that loneliness that has followed you
from birth
that sadness that creeps up on you
and drives you to literature
late at night

for the first time
that constant pain was lifted
and you understood
that existence can be
sweet

so then to be cast out
and returned to the ache
of knowing you are yet again
unknown and unknowable
to anyone, by anyone
you are yet again
imprisoned in your own
solitude
your own sadness
your own inescapable
milieu of
of what?
of nothingness

that's the loneliest feeling
in the world, kids

to know for the first time
what it is to be spared from
loneliness

and then
to be cast back into it

that'll tear you
so profoundly
you'll wish for death

and kids, I have to tell you that
you must resist that feeling
that beautiful pull
towards the third rail
the gorgeous allure
of headlights
the tantalizing pleasure
of bridges

I'm here to tell you

that loneliness
that horrible
horrible feeling that you right now
are holding so closely
you don't even realize it

you think it's a part of yourself
you think it's something like skin
you think of it as a condition
a natural side effect of life

that loneliness
when returned after a relief so sweet
you saw for the first time
it could be possible to have pleasure in your life

that loneliness
is an agony
so profound

I wouldn't wish it on my worst enemies

well, except maybe one

may she rot in hell
or Sacramento
—whichever burns worse

you got that, kids?

2.

(At the buffet.)

CARLY. so! how are you?

CARLO. I'm great.

CARLY. that's great! that's really good.
I heard through the grapevine you were going through
a rough patch

CARLO. grape vine,
rough patch:
good words.

CARLY. uh huh

CARLO. how's Sacramento?

CARLY. it's great

CARLO. that's great—
you know, Marly

CARLY. it's Carly

CARLO. Marly, I was surprised
to see your place in the ceremony
you were what? third in line?
I had my money on you being maid of honor

things must have changed in the last—
how long has it been?

CARLY. it's been a while, Carlo

CARLO. do not worry
I think you're the dark horse in the bridesmaid race
you'll be married next
I can feel it

CARLY. wasn't the ceremony beautiful?

CARLO. honestly?
> just between us gal-pals?
>
> did it seem aggressively heterosexual to you?
> like I almost thought they were going to start checking
> for her hymen
> right there in front of us

CARLY. I thought it was nice

CARLO. did you?
> I just kept thinking one stray drop of that holy water
> and bam
> my skin would start to sizzle
>
> or what if I was smited—smote?
> right there in the chapel—
> do you think that's the origin of the burning bush?
>
> somebody's lesbian ex just
> wooosh

CARLY. that's funny
> I wasn't thinking about myself at all

> (**CARLO** *resumes picking at the buffet.*)

CARLO. what is this?
> is there meat in this?
> why are there no labels on anything?
> what if I had a life-threatening allergy?

CARLY. do you?

CARLO. no, but it's the principle of the thing
> they could have a little respect for their guests, don't
> you think?

CARLY. I was surprised to see you here

CARLO. well, "some people grow apart,
> others stay close to the heart"
>
> I read that on a pillow once

CARLY. where are you seated?

CARLO. oh
I'm just sort of doing the rounds

CARLY. because I thought I saw you at the kids' table?

CARLO. wow, somebody is keeping tabs on me

CARLY. then there was a mass migration of children,
crying—
do you have any idea what happened there?

CARLO. no, and I am so interested in finding out

CARLY. are you sure you should be here tonight?

CARLO. are you sure *you* should be here tonight?

CARLY. I am very happy to be here celebrating someone I
love

CARLO. so am I

CARLY. are you?

CARLO. I am

CARLY. because, you know,
if you thought you could handle this,
and then you got here,
and you discovered that you weren't actually up for it,
it wouldn't be a failure if you decided to leave

it would actually be a sign of strength
of growth, even

that you removed yourself from a situation that you
couldn't handle

CARLO. okay,
I think you might be projecting a little, Marly

CARLY. Carly

CARLO. are you doing okay?
I know it's rough to be so publicly demoted

in the friendship chain

so if you need to leave,
no one here will judge you

I mean we'll all talk about it
but with *love* in our hearts

> (**VICTOR** *crosses holding a tray.*)

CARLY. I think you should leave

CARLO. I am being very pleasant!
you're the one making a scene

> (**CARLO** *tries to involve* **VICTOR.**)

I'm so sorry about her,
just go around us

> (**VICTOR** *ducks around them, exits.*)

CARLY. you made a table full of children cry!

CARLO. okay, that was one kid
and honestly?
he's probably the one who needed to hear it the most,
okay?

is that really your biggest argument—
Carlo cares too much about the children?

because I am fine with that
you can write that on my tombstone:
CARLO CARED FOR THE CHILDREN

CARLY. you have a funny way of caring for people,
don't you?

CARLO. you have a funny way of speaking to people,
don't you?

CARLY. should I call you a car?

CARLO. oh I see what's happening...

  are you trying to leave with me?

CARLY. my only interest in you
    is getting you out of here

CARLO. I know! stop trying to leave with me!!

  this is like that Spice Girls party all over again

CARLY. I was pretending to be Sporty Spice!!

CARLO. and you nailed it

CARLY. I'm just trying to make sure that
    no one loses focus on what this night is about

CARLO. good luck with that, Marly, honey
    it's so good to see you

3.

(At the bar.)

*(**VICTOR** is attempting to set up the bar.)*

ELI. whiskey neat, please

CARLO. same

*(**VICTOR** nods and exits for on offstage bottle.)*

ELI. I'm a little nervous

CARLO. I can tell

ELI. really?
   am I sweating?

CARLO. no, floral prints always scream anxiety

ELI. oh

CARLO. I'm kidding

ELI. I'm Eli

   sorry, I'm Eli
   no, sorry, I'm—

CARLO. Eli, I know

   what is it, your bar mitzvah?
   you're gonna do fine, kid

   just remember to breathe

ELI. no, I'm—
   I'm planning to propose tonight

CARLO. oh no
   no, no, no
   Eli, Eli, Eli
   do not propose at a wedding!
   are you kidding me?

ELI. no, I've got a whole plan
   the DJ is going to play a song
   and the ring bearer –

CARLO. that is considered emotionally hijacking an event
   and it is *frowned upon*

   my aunt once gave an unplanned toast at my sister's
   wedding
   and we're still unpacking that family trauma

   (**VICTOR** *delivers their drinks.*)

ELI. I think it could be really nice
   but I guess it wouldn't hurt to ask

CARLO. do not ask and do not do it, okay?

   besides no one likes public displays of affection

ELI. I don't know
   I kind of find them touching

CARLO. no, it's crude, trust me
   most people just have gaping voids where their hearts
   should be
   and public displays of affection really hit that home for
   us—
   so then we're forced to spend the rest of the night
   mocking you
   just so we can recover

   it's a whole thing

   and that will be what people leave this wedding talking
   about
   and whoopsie
   look at that
   the bride and groom hate you now
   they literally hate you

   what, you thought you were close?
   where are you in the seating radius?

ELI. table three

CARLO. oh wow
  you think you're inner circle, huh?

ELI. I'm practically family, the groom is—

CARLO. nope
  trust me, dead to them

  besides, literally no one wants to be proposed to in public
  except maybe sociopaths
  —or what's it called when you get off on being watched?

ELI. exhibitionists

CARLO. yeah, is your partner an exhibitionist?

ELI. they're not, no

CARLO. well, then, they would hate that

ELI. the whole family is here, I think—

CARLO. oh my god! even worse!
  can you imagine?

ELI. I can, yes, that's why

CARLO. no, oh my god, who wants to make out in front of their grandma?
  you into sick fucks, Eli?

ELI. they're a very nice person

CARLO. okay, so, pretty obviously a bad plan here, bud

ELI. you might be right

        (*To* **VICTOR**.)

CARLO. can we have another round, please?
  thank you

        (**VICTOR** *pops up and nods.*)

(He begins to make them more drinks.)

*(**CARLO** returns to **ELI**.)*

tell me more about your partner

ELI. they're the best

CARLO. yeah, yeah, yeah, smart and funny and cute
skip to the real stuff

ELI. okay, they're a graphic designer

CARLO. good eyebrows?

ELI. great eyebrows

CARLO. graphic designers always have incredible
eyebrows...

ELI. they look like they don't care about a single thing
like really...

CARLO. withholding?

ELI. no, like, um
stoic? or reserved

but underneath they care really deeply about
everything—
I haven't used a plastic bag since I met them

CARLO. okay, be careful,
I might fall in love too

*(**VICTOR** delivers their drinks.)*

ELI. I'm going to be honest
the first time their face lit up when they saw me
I went home and had a panic attack
I mean
I'm a high school English teacher
I'm meant for a small comedy of errors at most

CARLO. huh

ELI. I just mean that
I have never risked tragedy once in my entire life
it's not my genre
I know that about myself

I don't suffer well—
some people suffer very well!
they write epic poems or their skin sort of glows

when I'm sad

I just retain water
chronically

like my ankles swell?
I've taken a steroid before—
it's not pretty

CARLO. yikes

ELI. and so there was a moment when I almost
shot the albatross down from the sky

CARLO. ??

ELI. like the Ancient Mariner—
Coleridge?

CARLO. no idea what you're talking about

ELI. oh it's a wonderful poem
you should really—

CARLO. yeah, I'm not going to do that

ELI. what I mean is that
I almost couldn't recognize the miracle
that was entering my life
I almost shot it out of the sky
just because I was afraid

but instead
they noticed that I was starting to withdraw,
and they just leaned into me and said

"risk joy, Eli"

and that was it, wasn't it?

because they're two sides of the same coin
joy and pain—right?

to risk one, you risk the other?

CARLO. wow this got earnest, didn't it

ELI. I'm sorry, I—

CARLO. no, it's my fault
weddings are a minefield for earnest contemplation
I should have crashed a funeral instead

>   *(To* **VICTOR***:)*

can we get another round, please?
thank you

>   *(Back to* **ELI***:)*

Eli, darling, love of my life—

—do not propose tonight.
and if I can just give one blanket piece of advice to
heterosexuals:

>   *(***CARLO** *pauses to look at* **VICTOR**
>   *questioningly:)*

>   *(***VICTOR** *non-verbally confirms that he is
>   gay.)*

learn how to say all these weird things to the person
you love
and not the person you meet at the bar

>   *(***VICTOR** *hands drinks to* **CARLO** *and* **ELI***.)*

cheers!

4.

(At the high top.)

MARIA. Carlo oh thank god
    someone interesting

CARLO. Maria

MARIA. you didn't RSVP—you scoundrel

CARLO. sorry

MARIA. it's fine, my date cancelled last minute
    e.coli, he's fine
    did you hear Toby brought someone?

CARLO. I didn't

MARIA. I bet she's half his age
    so this works out quite nicely then
    you'll be my date

CARLO. oh I don't know if I should

MARIA. don't be a bore, darling
    it's not your strong suit

CARLO. right

MARIA. what did you think of the ceremony?

    *(**CARLO** makes a face.)*

see? this is why I like you

    *(**VICTOR** starts to cross with a drink tray.)*

here, come on, drink something with me

    *(**MARIA** grabs two drinks from **VICTOR**'s
    tray.)*

protect me from this hell

(MARIA turns back to cheers CARLO.)

(But CARLO also grabs two drinks off of VICTOR's tray.)

(They double cheers.)

cheers!

so how are you
it's been too long – why don't you ever come to see me?
are you seeing someone?

CARLO. no, I'm

MARIA. oh that's good, honey
"hell is other people"
my mother used to say that
"hell is other people, Maria –
never get married"
I should have listened to her

CARLO. I'm glad you didn't

MARIA. you are? why?

oh, right
well you know some snakes reproduce by themselves
if they're isolated for too long
they just birth a little sliver of their own DNA—
a little clone!
just like the virgin Mary

CARLO. wow,
we have been reading different texts

MARIA. I'm just saying
maybe I could have skipped the miserable marriage
and hatched Eva instead
I can't believe he brought a date—
do you think they're serious?

CARLO. I don't know—
    are you and e.coli serious?

MARIA. who? oh no
    he's my butcher
    gives me discount meats

CARLO. romantic

MARIA. at a certain age, honey
    you know so much more about what you don't want
    than what you do want—
    mostly I want to be left alone

CARLO. I can already hear the toast

MARIA. she didn't ask me to speak
    but I think I might say something
    contemporaneously

CARLO. you *definitely* should

MARIA. maybe we should give a little tag-team toast

CARLO. Maria, I would love nothing more
    than to drink three more of these—

MARIA. just three? what are you, sober?

CARLO. I've missed you

MARIA. oh honey I've missed *you*
    I'm afraid Eva's gone square

CARLO. I'm not sure about square but definitely straight

MARIA. what do you think of him

CARLO. who

MARIA. the groom

CARLO. I don't think of him, actually
    as a general rule

    even now I'm sure I've seen him before

MARIA. he played a big role in the ceremony

CARLO. and yet I can't quite bring a face to mind
he's just a blank in my—

MARIA. I think you're onto something, actually
he's sort of boring

dependable, stable, even-keeled

CARLO. not your type

MARIA. not even a little

even Toby had his flare for the dramatic

CARLO. he must have

MARIA. did I ever tell you about our honeymoon?

CARLO. maybe, but tell me again

MARIA. he took me camping

CARLO. this was back in your Birkenstock days?

MARIA. I did a lot of things to the sound of Joni Mitchell...

CARLO. okay, we can skip the hairy details

MARIA. and they *were* hairy
although we called it *au naturel*

CARLO. I am going to need another drink

MARIA. my whole family said
"you're taking *Maria* camping?"

but it was a different time

my hair was down to my ass;
I wore a flower crown at the ceremony

and on the very first night
of the honeymoon

we went for a hike
and we came across a river

and we took our clothes off
and we got in the water

and Toby reached out to touch me
in the moonlight

but as he stretched out his hand,
he noticed the water was glimmering
with little gold flecks

and his eyes got wide
—he was not entirely sober—
and he just started screaming

GOLD
WE'VE STRUCK GOLD

and he jumped out of the river
and he started pulling on his pants
and he said:

"okay, this is very important
you've got to hike back to camp
and call my brother, Andy

tell him we've found gold,
and he needs to get some equipment
and come meet me

I'll stay here and guard it—
do not tell a single soul!!!!"

and so I started pulling on my clothes
—I was not exactly sober myself—
and just then a man walked by and
I swear to god
Toby saw him and yelled

"HEY! WE FOUND GOLD!"

and the man walked up,
put his hand in the river

and said "pyrite"
and walked off

CARLO. what's pyrite?

MARIA. fool's gold
that became a little joke between us
when Toby was first working on his startup
he'd tell me an idea, and if it was bad, I'd say
"pyrite"

does she look young?

CARLO. who?

MARIA. his date

CARLO. I didn't see her

MARIA. well, fuck him, right?

CARLO. right

MARIA. fuck 'em all, am I right?

CARLO. now you're speaking my language, Maria

MARIA. I always liked you

CARLO. thanks

MARIA. I fought for you, you know

CARLO. really?

MARIA. oh yeah

I said what about Carlo
I liked Carlo

CARLO. what did she say?

MARIA. she said "I know you did"
and she smiled

she can be a real *bitch*, you know that?

CARLO. okay,

let's not go down this road, Maria

MARIA. I bet Toby is giving a speech

CARLO. we'll give ours after, it'll be a hoot

MARIA. I'm not dancing with the groom, nothing

CARLO. you can dance with me

MARIA. sometimes I think she doesn't even like me

CARLO. she loves you, Maria

> (**VICTOR** *starts to cross with empty glasses.*)

MARIA. yeah, well,
would it kill her to like me

> (**MARIA** *flags* **VICTOR**.)

can we get two more of these, please

CARLO. I think you need a dance break
c'mon, let's go dance

MARIA. maybe later

CARLO. Maria

MARIA. go on, go

CARLO. ?

MARIA. you want to go,
get the hell out of here

CARLO. I wasn't trying to leave

MARIA. fuck off, Carlo

5.

(On the roof.)

LEIGH. what are you doing way up here?

CARLO. just getting some air

LEIGH. not enough air for you in the garden

CARLO. no, this is the good stuff

LEIGH. it does seem better quality

CARLO. see?

it's airier
somehow

LEIGH. mind if I smoke?

CARLO. you left the mediocre air just to smoke in the good stuff?

LEIGH. sure did

CARLO. go ahead

(**LEIGH** *lights the cigarette and smokes.)*

(**LEIGH** *offers* **CARLO** *a drag.)*

(**CARLO** *takes a drag and then passes it back.)*

no thanks, I don't smoke
I want to die in a much more fantastic way
I have to be careful not to waste my death
on something so mundane

LEIGH. which fantastic way

CARLO. like in some glorious
blaze of death

I'm still working out the details

LEIGH. like a car crash

CARLO. no, no, no
      like setting myself on fire in a public square

LEIGH. I see, more spectacle

CARLO. oh spectacle is very important
      I think
      I think there should be an eloquence to it

      like now for instance
      if I were to die right now

      I'd like to sort of careen off the roof into the party
      land spine first on the gift table

      like: "take this body, my last gift to you"

LEIGH. it's a little dramatic

CARLO. you think that's dramatic?

LEIGH. yeah it's like obviously you want to traumatize
      everyone

CARLO. huh

LEIGH. I feel like it should be much more mysterious
      like you should just fling yourself off a cliff
      and that will be the spectacle:

      "one day she was fine, a guest at a wedding,
      the next they were pulling her body in with a net...
      no one even knew she was sad."

CARLO. that won't work

LEIGH. why not?

CARLO. everyone knows I'm sad

LEIGH. hm

      it'd have to be a long con then

you'd have to put a lot of energy into faking happiness
first

CARLO. they say faking happiness can actually make you
happy
like smiling can somehow—

LEIGH. people say a lot of stupid shit

CARLO. what was your name again?

LEIGH. Leigh

CARLO. Carlo

LEIGH. Hi Carlo

CARLO. Hi Leigh

LEIGH. should we get out of here?

CARLO. where should we go?

LEIGH. I don't know
a bar, the ocean, the bluffs

CARLO. the bluffs, huh?

how do I know you're not planning on taking me to my
death?
how do I know you're not going to push me off the cliffs
and say I jumped?

LEIGH. you don't, I guess

isn't that part of the allure?

CARLO. sort of

LEIGH. you have no idea if I'm going to murder you
or sleep with you

CARLO. or cannibalize me!!!

are you a cannibal?!

LEIGH. who knows?

CARLO. you know, there is a theory
　　　that our complete saturation in technology
　　　combined with our absurd
　　　overexposure to violence
　　　is actually responsible for the recent rise
　　　in um
　　　cannibalism—

　　　don't you think that's interesting?

LEIGH. huh

CARLO. like normal bloodlust has become so passé
　　　you can't turn on the television without seeing someone
　　　being flayed alive
　　　so now the people who might normally have been
　　　satisfied with normal murder
　　　need to like eat people to get that same high

　　　and intimacy
　　　what is intimacy
　　　anymore

　　　no one knows
　　　people are just eating each other now...

LEIGH. now I'm starting to think you're a cannibal

CARLO. what do you think that's like?

LEIGH. cannibalism?

CARLO. like do you think people know that they have this
　　　weird craving for human flesh
　　　and they carry it around with them all the time
　　　like they wake up in the morning and look at themselves
　　　in the mirror
　　　and they're like:
　　　"you can do this,
　　　just another day of not eating people.
　　　you got this, Brian."

until one day they can't?

do you think there are lots of would-be-cannibals
who just manage to suppress their taboo feelings?

LEIGH. I doubt it
I bet it's more crime of passion-y

like you're stabbing someone to death
and the adrenaline is so kicked up
that you bite their face off

CARLO. what about the ones who plot to kill and cook the
people they love?
what about them?

LEIGH. "I loved her so much, I had to eat her"

CARLO. "I wanted to consume her.
Literally."

LEIGH. I can almost understand it

CARLO. yeah
me too

LEIGH. shall we?

CARLO. hm?

LEIGH. get out of here?

CARLO. oh

um

I think I'm actually going to stick around for a little
longer

LEIGH. okay, well, it was nice meeting you

CARLO. you too

6.

(In a supply closet.)

*(**CARLO** is lost.)*

*(**VICTOR** is cleaning something up.)*

*(But just as **CARLO** is about to get **VICTOR**'s attention.)*

(His phone rings.)

VICTOR. hey baby

no, I'm still here
Tony called out, so it's a fucking mess
and Joe got wasted before we even got to cocktail hour
so they have me covering the bar ??
like hello
I hope that means I am getting Joe's cut

of course not

I did!

I mean I said it
but I think they thought I was kidding

I will, I will

I know

ugh I'm exhausted

how you feeling? does it still itch?
did you pick up that cream?

try just sitting in the bath.
warm water should... shrink them.

I saved you some of those crab cakes

ha. I'll try

okay, I better go
god forbid someone not get their canapé

I love you too

> *(**VICTOR** hangs up.)*

> *(**CARLO** approaches and accidentally startles* **VICTOR**.*)*

CARLO. sorry

VICTOR. whoa

CARLO. your boyfriend seems...

nice

VICTOR. he's my other half

need something?

CARLO. I'm a little lost

VICTOR. party's that way

CARLO. thank you,

> *(**CARLO** reads **VICTOR**'s name tag.)*

Victor

7.

(On the dance floor.)

EVA. Carlo

CARLO. Eva

EVA. you made it

CARLO. wouldn't miss it

EVA. I wasn't sure—
you didn't RSVP

CARLO. didn't I?
that's weird
it must have gotten lost in the mail
or something

EVA. it's okay,
I'm just happy you're here

CARLO. you look
amazing

EVA. thank you
I see you're wearing the wedding outfit

CARLO. tried and true
never failed

EVA. you look good,
are you good?

CARLO. I'm good,
I'm great

EVA. that's great

CARLO. how about you?
how are you?

EVA. I'm getting married

CARLO. I noticed

EVA. no,
　　I am married

CARLO. Wow

EVA. I'm married—
　　that's very weird to say

CARLO. it's very weird to hear

　　what's this playlist

EVA. don't

CARLO. no I like it
　　it's

EVA. stop

CARLO. what?
　　you don't even know what I'm going to say

EVA. I can guess

CARLO. see that's where you're wrong
　　it's been a while, Eva

　　who knows I might be
　　an entirely different person now

EVA. oh yeah?

CARLO. yeah

　　can't you tell

EVA. I think that might be the alcohol

CARLO. oh c'mon
　　look at me:

　　I feel great

EVA. it's much more convincing
　　when you're not yelling about it

CARLO. am I yelling?

EVA. "I FEEL GREAT"

CARLO. ME TOO
  I FEEL GREAT

EVA. EVERYTHING IS WONDERFUL

CARLO. EVERYTHING IS FUCKING FANTASTIC

EVA. THIS IS EXACTLY WHAT I'VE ALWAYS WANTED

CARLO. is it?

EVA. yeah

CARLO. this?

EVA. this

CARLO. you're happy?

EVA. I'm exhausted
  wedding planning is exactly as bad
  as everyone says it is

CARLO. right, but

  are you happy?

EVA. I'm hungry too
  they say you don't get to eat
  at your own wedding
  and that's true
  that's also true
  did you get to eat,
  what did you eat?

CARLO. I had some finger food—
  I don't know
  it wasn't labeled

EVA. it wasn't labeled?!
  what if someone had a life-threatening allergy?!

CARLO. I know, I know
but I haven't seen a single person
in anaphylactic shock,
so you're probably okay

EVA. I should go talk to the caterer—

CARLO. no, no, no
you should talk to me
stay with me

EVA. Carlo

CARLO. dance with me

EVA. I really probably should not

you should probably eat something
and I should probably find my way to the other guests

CARLO. I read somewhere that the bride is supposed to
dance with every guest as her wedding

EVA. that can't be true

CARLO. it's what I read
Miss Manners I think
something very proper

you wouldn't want to be rude, would you Eva?

EVA. oh, shut up

CARLO. c'mon
we always have a blast at weddings

EVA. did we?
I remember you always wanting to leave

CARLO. yeah, but it's always fun
we had a lot of fun

do you remember Kendall's wedding?

EVA. *(Teasing.)* I forgot that you always cry at weddings did you cry at my wedding?

CARLO. not yet

EVA. well, there's still time

CARLO. I'll be honest
yours has been kind of tame

EVA. I think the word you're looking for is
drama-free

CARLO. no, I meant boring

EVA. you know what?
I cut all the drama out of my life
and I sleep like a baby these days

CARLO. oh good
so you were hoping to give off a deep coma vibe
in that case:
mission accomplished

EVA. *(Playfully.)* you are such an asshole

CARLO. it's not too late, you know
if you want to shake it up a little
give 'em something to talk about

EVA. oh yeah,
what do you have in mind?

CARLO. well, I mean
it could go any number of ways
you've got a couple ticking time bombs at this wedding
and to be honest
I've been neutralizing the situations
out of respect for you
and your new boring life

but I could always throw a little gasoline on the fire
if you want

EVA. I'm trying to decide if I want to know

what you're talking about

CARLO. you do, don't you?

EVA. my head says no

CARLO. I'm not talking to your head, Eva
when have I ever been talking to your head?

EVA. *(Despite herself, hungry for the gossip.)* tell me

CARLO. well the first option is
there's this douchebag who wants to propose to his partner
at your wedding

EVA. are you fucking kidding me

CARLO. that's what I said!
I said that would be unforgivable
absolutely despicable

but if you want it,
I could probably make that happen

EVA. why would I want that?

CARLO. well, to be honest,
I'm looking around
and I'm starting to think this wedding needs a villain
something to bring us all closer together
a bonding experience for the guests
and he's more of a patsy
but he'd get the job done

EVA. no

CARLO. okay, I figured you'd say that
so the next option is a long shot
but a certain bridesmaid
seems like she could go Black Swan at any moment

EVA. stop it!
she does not!

CARLO. you know she does

EVA. I do not understand why you two have always hated
each other

CARLO. so she does hate me!
you always said she didn't

EVA. no, she has always hated your guts
and please do not set her off

CARLO. okay, well there's—
no,
let's not go there

EVA. what?

CARLO. no no no
forget I said it

EVA. no, I can't
you have to tell me

CARLO. your mom

EVA. okay, I changed my mind
I don't want to know

CARLO. right

EVA. she's okay though, right?

CARLO. right

EVA. you promise?

CARLO. I mean
she's Maria
she came in her own armor

EVA. my dad's new partner
is actually really nice

CARLO. I'm sure!
she seems like a great girl

EVA. she's not as young as she looks

CARLO. oh thank god

> (*They both share a real laugh at this.*)
>
> (*The laughter brings them closer together physically – a hand on a knee or a squeezed arm – the intimacy is easy and natural and feels good.*)
>
> (*And then it lingers, becoming tempting and dangerous.*)
>
> (*Eventually* **EVA** *breaks it.*)

EVA. okay, well
if those are all the options
I think I'll keep my boring wedding intact

CARLO. well there is one more option
but
it's nuclear

EVA. what is it?

CARLO. people would never forget it
this wedding would go down in history
years and years later people would be saying:
"did you hear what happened
at Eva's wedding?"

EVA. What?

CARLO. you could leave with me

EVA. because my wedding is too boring?

CARLO. sure

or because that's what you want
that's what you actually want

EVA. Carlo

CARLO. c'mon Eva
　　　this whole thing is a farce
　　　what is this?

　　　I've seen more convincing fire drills

EVA. stop

CARLO. no, I'm serious
　　　you don't have to do this

EVA. you just watched me take my vows

CARLO. vows what are vows
　　　who cares about vows

　　　you didn't sign the paper yet did you

EVA. I did

CARLO. that's fine
　　　we'll get it annulled

EVA. Carlo

CARLO. I made a mistake, Eva

EVA. I can't do this right now

CARLO. I'm sorry

EVA. why are you doing this?

CARLO. because this can't be how it ends

EVA. it ended a long time ago, Carlo

　　　I gave you a year to do this

CARLO. you did?

EVA. I thought if she can prove that

　　　she's changed

CARLO. I have!
　　　I've changed, I've grown,
　　　I've

EVA. if she apologizes

CARLO. I'm sorry, Eva
I'm truly sorry

EVA. without me asking

if she can name what she did wrong

CARLO. well, that's pretty obvious, isn't?

EVA. is it?

CARLO. if I said it was a mistake, would you believe me?

EVA. no

CARLO. if I said I was happy I woke up, would you believe
me?

EVA. no

CARLO. please just let me explain—

EVA. you had so many chances
this isn't one of them

CARLO. I didn't know there was a deadline

EVA. so it's my fault?

CARLO. no, of course not

EVA. I should go, or
you should go

CARLO. let's go together

EVA. no

CARLO. you can't lie to me
I know you to well
this isn't you
you don't want this

EVA. I do I want this

CARLO. no, you don't

there's no way in hell
you want this

this is a major over-correction

I feel like I've been invited to your lobotomy

EVA. fuck you

CARLO. I'm sorry
I'm sorry
that was too harsh

I just mean

every day with you was the best day of my life

EVA. except for when it was the worst

tell me something
how much have you had to drink tonight?

CARLO. one drink

EVA. ha

CARLO. maybe two
I'm really cutting back, Eva
I'm serious

EVA. oh yeah?

CARLO. yes

EVA. where are you working these days?

CARLO. who cares?
are you serious, Eva?
you're what?
you're marrying for money?
that's
that's really sad
I feel sorry for you

EVA. right back atcha, babe

it's not about money
it's about someone who doesn't lie to me
about how much they're drinking
someone who can commit to what they're doing
next week, next month, next year
someone who loves themself
so they're not just draining me

CARLO. why did you invite me
If this isn't what you wanted

why did you invite me
if you didn't want me to save you

EVA. did you ever consider for single moment

that I wanted you to be happy for me

CARLO. I'm sorry

EVA. I'm not,
I'm glad

CARLO. you are?

EVA. I'm where I want to be

CARLO. you mean –

EVA. I mean
without you

I'm building a life
this is what that looks like

sometimes its really fucking boring

I hope you have a boring life one day
I really want that for you

CARLO. me too
I want it
and I could do it
I could do it for you

I could do it with you

EVA. no, baby, not with me

8.

(In the bathroom.)

*(**CARLO** is alone, looking in the mirror, not doing well.)*

*(**CARLY** exits the bathroom stall.)*

CARLY. hey

CARLO. hi

CARLY. you doing okay?

CARLO. great
  I'm doing great

CARLY. great

CARLO. I'm doing fantastic

CARLY. okay

CARLO. I'm happy for her

CARLY. yeah?

CARLO. so happy
  succulents
  name cards
  mason jars

  that's a wedding, alright
  that's a fucking wedding

CARLY. yeah

CARLO. or do you know what?

CARLY. what

CARLO. do you know what a wedding is

CARLY. why don't you tell me

CARLO. she looked at my grandmother
and she said
"so that's what you'll look like when you're old"
and then she kissed me

that was a wedding

this is just—

> *(**CARLO** starts to cry.)*

> *(**CARLY** approaches her cautiously.)*

> *(She holds her.)*

> *(**CARLO** resists and then doesn't.)*

> *(It calms her.)*

9.

(At the gift table.)

*(**VICTOR** is trying to cross with a multi-tiered wedding cake.)*

*(The cake is as big as **VICTOR**.)*

*(It seems certain **VICTOR** will drop it.)*

*(**CARLO** watches.)*

*(Eventually, **VICTOR** successfully crosses.)*

*(**CARLO** stares at the gift table.)*

*(**LEIGH** enters.)*

LEIGH. you're still here

CARLO. you too

LEIGH. got caught heading for the door

what are you doing?

CARLO. why do they call it a white elephant?

LEIGH. I'm not sure

but you do know *this* isn't a white elephant, right?
this is just the gift table
for the bride and groom

CARLO. I'm not sure

LEIGH. no, I'm telling you, it isn't

CARLO. elephant in the room
white elephant

if I am the elephant in the room
do I make all gift tables into white elephants

by like
existing?

LEIGH. probably not, no

and what makes you think you're the elephant in the
room?

CARLO. the bride's my ex

LEIGH. I think there were a lot of exes here

CARLO. really?

LEIGH. yeah

my brother's ex was here

CARLO. your brother?

LEIGH. the groom

CARLO. oh god

LEIGH. yeah

CARLO. what's he like?

LEIGH. I don't know

CARLO. you don't know

LEIGH. not really
I mean
he's my brother so
I hate him and I love him
and I have no idea who he is

CARLO. right

LEIGH. what's she like?

CARLO. I don't know

LEIGH. you don't know

CARLO. she's my ex so
I hate her and I love her

and I have no idea who she is

LEIGH. makes sense

CARLO. I really have no god damn idea who she is

look at all these presents
what are these?
look at this stupid party

sorry, is that—

LEIGH. no, it is pretty stupid

CARLO. did they feed each other cake too?
like some terrible hetero charade?
like "we're married now so we can't eat cake by
ourselves"

who the hell is she even?

LEIGH. I don't really know

CARLO. I think it *is* a white elephant
I think one of these gifts is meant for me

I think if I pick the right gift off this table,
the whole rest of my life will just sort of open up

like if I get a kitchen-aid
I'll know I'm supposed to take better care of myself
but if I get a towel set
it means I'm supposed to indulge more

LEIGH. is that what a towel set means?

CARLO. wedding presents
such a fucking joke
they're already happy
they're already adults
they have fucking utensils
two whole sets probably

you know when they should give you presents?

divorce
because that's when you realize you don't have any
mixing bowls
that's when you find yourself suddenly eating soup out
of mug
and it doesn't feel cute

there's nothing romantic about an empty house
when it doesn't feel like a beginning
when it feels like an end

I hope they got a prenup
that's when you want to figure everything out
when you still love each other

LEIGH. so I'm getting that you're a romantic...

CARLO. I think maybe this one is calling to me

it's small
no one will miss it

LEIGH. I don't know—
looking for a message
in random things

do you turn on the radio and assume all the songs are
about you?

CARLO. one hundred percent
yes

what's the alternative?

LEIGH. you know
making your own decisions
taking responsibility for your actions
not seeing yourself as a victim of a random universe
but as an active player in your own life

CARLO. hm
that's an interesting way of looking at the world
I've never thought of that

but
if I do it my way
I get a present right now

and that seems nice

>   (**CARLO** *picks up a small present.*)

LEIGH. are you sure it's that one?
that's the one that's going to tell you how to live your
life?

CARLO. yeah,
I can just sort of feel it
the universe is telling me
this is the one

LEIGH. open it

>   (**CARLO** *opens a small present from the gift
>   table.*)
>
>   (*It's a terrible empty photo frame with an
>   inscription.*)

CARLO. shit
who gives someone an empty photo frame?

>   (**CARLO** *passes it to* **LEIGH** *who reads the
>   inscription:*)

LEIGH. "My Favorite Love Story is Ours"

what's it tell you?

CARLO. that my life is a cruel joke

LEIGH. maybe it's telling you to fill the frame
no more empty space

CARLO. maybe

LEIGH. come on,
let's get out of here

CARLO. why?

LEIGH. what?

CARLO. let's say we did
let's say we walked out that door
and we had the best night of our lives

then what?
it never ends well

LEIGH. first tell me about the best night of our lives
then I'll tell you about the
then what

CARLO. we sneak out through the kitchen
grabbing a bottle of champagne as we slip by

LEIGH. and half the cake

CARLO. half?!

LEIGH. I get hungry when I drink

CARLO. alright, half.
and we take the cake—
where do we take it?

LEIGH. to the dive down the street
called The Golden West

CARLO. I love The Golden West

LEIGH. we share the cake with everyone in the bar,
which makes us wildly popular
we drink a few rounds for free

CARLO. rounds of what

LEIGH. tequila

CARLO. oooo
this is going to hurt tomorrow

LEIGH. but we're not worried about tomorrow

because
just then an announcement flashes
on the shitty bar television

CARLO. breaking news

LEIGH. the world is officially ending
this is our last night on earth

so we lean over the juke box

CARLO. there's no juke box at The Golden West

LEIGH. pretend there's a juke box

CARLO. oh *that* juke box

LEIGH. and we put on all the best songs
for an impending apocalypse

CARLO. and we dance

LEIGH. we're very close together

CARLO. until it's later than either of us imagined
and then we grab our bottle of champagne

LEIGH. we didn't drink that already?

CARLO. no, no, no,
we've been drinking tequila
we've been saving the champagne

LEIGH. for what

CARLO. for this—
we walk all the way down Redwood
all the way to the beach

LEIGH. that street is still fenced off

CARLO. we climb the fence

LEIGH. I'm terrible at climbing

CARLO. I give you a boost

LEIGH. you're not very strong

CARLO. wait, no, look—
a hole in the fence
just over here

LEIGH. we climb through it

CARLO. it scrapes

LEIGH. I kiss your scrapes

CARLO. we keep walking
down to the beach

LEIGH. the sand is cold
the water is freezing

CARLO. there's a significant amount of driftwood
an alarming amount

LEIGH. we build a makeshift structure

CARLO. for our last night on earth

LEIGH. we open the champagne

CARLO. but we don't drink it

LEIGH. why not?

CARLO. because we've started kissing

LEIGH. have we?

CARLO. we've started kissing
and we can't stop

LEIGH. we take our clothes off

CARLO. the sand is cold

LEIGH. I don't notice the sand

CARLO. god you look good in moonlight

LEIGH. so do you

(**CARLO** *and* **LEIGH** *kiss.*)

CARLO. shit

LEIGH. what?

CARLO. suddenly I'm sad

LEIGH. why are you sad?

CARLO. I'm bereft

LEIGH. why?

CARLO. I wish it wasn't the last night on earth

LEIGH. wait, look

CARLO. what?

LEIGH. just over the ocean—
the sun is coming up

CARLO. no, that's worse

LEIGH. is it?

CARLO. yes, the only thing worse than the end of the world
is surviving it

thank you though
for a great night

LEIGH. we haven't had it yet

CARLO. I have, it was wonderful
you're...

LEIGH. stop, hold on, look at me:

take a risk, Carlo

risk joy

CARLO. you're not a graphic designer by any chance are
you?

LEIGH. how did you know that?

CARLO. are you fucking kidding me

LEIGH. what?

CARLO. I started the night by taking shots with your fiancé

LEIGH. I don't have a fiancé

CARLO. good luck telling Eli that

LEIGH. we're open

CARLO. okay, great, good luck with all that

LEIGH. why are you being so judgmental all of a sudden?

CARLO. I'm just really annoyed
    that you're making me
    empathize with a straight man right now

LEIGH. he's not straight
    we're very queer

CARLO. okay—noted.

    that's not actually the point
    the point is

    that guy
    that stupid little man in the floral shirt
    breaks my fucking heart
    with how he loves you, okay

    so if you don't love him—

LEIGH. of course I love him
    just because we're not monogamous doesn't mean—

CARLO. tell me about him

LEIGH. he's like the nicest person I've ever met

CARLO. yeah, yeah, yeah, he's nice, he's funny, he's cute
    whatever
    tell me the real stuff

LEIGH. that is the real stuff

CARLO. what's his genre?

LEIGH. what?

CARLO. if he was a book, what would his genre be?

LEIGH. that's a weird question

CARLO. just answer it!

LEIGH. I don't know!
he'd be witty non-fiction

CARLO. that's kind of a good answer actually—
it's not what I was thinking, but

LEIGH. what were you thinking?

CARLO. he said he was a small comedy of errors
risking tragedy

LEIGH. what?

CARLO. I don't know, he's your fiancé!

LEIGH. he's not my fiancé!

look, we've been together for like six years
some of it is just eating your vegetables at this point

CARLO. he's not eating his vegetables

LEIGH. he is! he puts in the work

CARLO. no, I mean
he's having a four-course meal with dessert

if you're eating your vegetables
do me a favor
and just break his heart

LEIGH. you don't know anything about us

CARLO. you've been trying to leave with me all night!

LEIGH. don't flatter yourself, babe
this party sucks

CARLO. I met Eli for like five minutes
and I care more about his feelings than you do right
now

LEIGH. that's bullshit
you don't know him

CARLO. neither do you, babe

it's a fucking tragedy

10.

*(**CARLO** goes back to the bar.)*

CARLO. hey

VICTOR. hey

CARLO. can I get another drink

> *(As if suddenly gripped by an ancient and mysterious force:)*

VICTOR. "water, water everywhere
and not a drop to drink"

CARLO. what?

> *(Back to normal:)*

VICTOR. let me check the back

> *(**VICTOR** exits.)*

11.

(On the dance floor.)

ELI. hey stranger!

CARLO. hey

this party sucks doesn't it?

ELI. I think it's kind of nice

CARLO. no, it's boring
let's go to a real bar

ELI. why would we leave an open bar?

CARLO. you make a good point

ELI. you missed a few choreographed dances

CARLO. this whole party makes me want to die

ELI. we just need to find you a nice person
weddings are a great place to meet people

CARLO. not so great, really

ELI. well, you've met me

CARLO.

ELI. thank you for talking me out of making a fool of
myself earlier

I'm going to propose where we met
that's better, right?
simpler?

CARLO. you are in some deep shit, my friend
and you don't even know it
you don't even realize it

that's what breaks my heart

you think they love you?

they're an amazon my friend
and you
what are you

they're a redwood
and you're a banana slug

it's never gonna work out

that's why I can't move on
because
I recognize you

yes, that's right I recognize you

it's a dark night of the soul for you
and you don't even know it

but I've seen it
I am your future

run
please
run

I'm begging you

because it's a long time
life
it's a very long time

it's a life sentence, really
and you can do it
alone
in theory
but I think the trick to it is
you can't know
the alternative

you can't have met the love of your life
and lost them

that's too much

I want to spare you that

so trust me
run
run now

>   (**VICTOR** *brings water to* **ELI** *for* **CARLO**.)

ELI. okay, here, hold on,

have you had any food tonight?

CARLO. I don't know

>   (*To* **VICTOR**.)

ELI. can we get some of those crab cakes, please?

>   (*Back to* **CARLO**.)

okay, I'm going to tell you a story
while you drink that water

CARLO. don't condescend me

ELI. sorry,
it's the story of the albatross
I think you should know it

>   (*Throughout this story* **ELI** *continually fills*
>   **CARLO***'s water glass.*)

>   (**VICTOR** *brings her canapés.*)

the poem takes place at a wedding

but we never actually make it to the wedding
because first we meet this crazed person
who won't stop
telling us the story he thinks we need to hear

so instead of going to the actual wedding
we're trapped all night

just outside of it
with this mariner

CARLO. what's a mariner

VICTOR. a seamen?

CARLO. ew

ELI. a sailor

CARLO. where's the boat

ELI. okay, so in the mariner's story
there's a boat
that gets lost at sea
completely stuck with no way forward

until one day an albatross appears
and saves them by guiding the boat
through this maze of fog and ice

it's a miracle
this bird
everyone on the boat would be dead without it

until one guy
our guy, our mariner,
he picks up his crossbow and shoots it

CARLO. why did he do that

ELI. have you ever been scared of a really good thing?

CARLO.

ELI. so he shoots the albatross
and the winds immediately stop
stranding them and then
sea monsters start circling the ship

and all the other boat guys are furious
so they make him
wear the albatross around his neck

so that he can't forget what he's done
it hangs there on his shoulders
weighing him down
day after day

and this is a huge bird by the way –
like an eleven foot wingspan

CARLO. like a dinosaur?

ELI. um… kind of?
I mean they're real
they're alive – endangered but alive

CARLO. what the hell
where do all these big birds live

ELI. I don't know

but listen
the sailors all die
except
the ancient mariner

he's all alone
with the albatross still wrapped around his neck
reminding him that it's all his fault, right?
all of it

he's trapped with that

and circling him in the water
are the sea monsters

he stares at them

until he realizes that they aren't
monsters waiting to devour him
they're actually beautiful
like the albatross was

he stops *fearing* them.
he feels love for them.

and he gives them each his blessing

and just like that
the albatross falls from his neck

CARLO. what about all the dead people?
do they come back?

ELI. no, they're dead

CARLO. and the bird, is it alive now?

ELI. no, it's still dead

CARLO. so he's saved
but everything he's ruined
still stays ruined?

ELI. I mean technically he's cursed
he's got a strange curse

CARLO. what's the curse?

ELI. whenever he sees the face of someone who needs to
hear his story
he has to tell it

which is why we're at the wedding
he's encountered someone who needs to hear his story

CARLO. I think he should suffer more

ELI. why?

CARLO. because all of those people died!
because he shot the bird!

ELI. but what would his suffering change?

CARLO. you don't get to be happy
when you've done so many bad things
so many stupid things

he should jump off the ship

ELI. what would that change?

just more blood on his hands

CARLO. so, what are trying to tell me?

that I just need to feel love in my heart
and that'll heal me?

do you think I've never heard that before?
do you think I've never tried that?

ELI. I don't know

CARLO. what if he forgets his lesson
and he shoots another bird?

ELI. but that's why he's got the curse

CARLO. pft that curse...
what if no one listens to his story
because they think he's out of his mind
because he sounds like a drunk
even when he's maybe making a lot of sense
even when he's the smartest person in the room
people think he's just a fucking drunk
and so they just close their hearts to him
just like that every door closes in his face somehow
what about that

ELI. I don't think the mariner drank at all in the story

CARLO. yeah, well, good for him

ELI. I mean at it's heart
it's a Christian redemption story

CARLO. boo

ELI. I don't believe in all that

to me, the story is about perception
the mariner can't recognize
miracles from monsters
because he's so gripped by fear

CARLO. there are monsters though

ELI. not in this story

CARLO. yeah, but they exist

ELI. do they?

CARLO. yes, I've met them
I've been them

not everyone can be saved

ELI. I think they can

> (**CARLO** *and* **ELI** *sit in that for a moment.*)

> (*Then* **ELI** *checks his phone.*)

oh I gotta go
my partner got us an Uber

good luck, man

CARLO. yeah, you too
sorry I called you a banana slug

ELI. it's okay,
I am a banana slug!
UC Santa Cruz—
go slugs!

I'll see you around

CARLO. you will never see me again in your life

ELI. no, I probably won't
it was fun though
weird but fun

goodnight

> (**ELI** *exits.*)

> (**CARLO** *sits in that until.*)

(Eventually **EVA** *enters.)*

CARLO. hey sorry can I—

EVA. can we just leave it for the night?
   it's my wedding

CARLO. yes, of course,
   I'm so sorry about—

   I'm sorry
   I'm leaving

   I just wanted to say:

   congratulations
   you deserve everything you ever wanted
   and I'm so happy you got it

   I really am

EVA. thank you

   does this mean we can finally be friends?

CARLO. when were we ever not friends?

EVA. I'm serious, be serious

CARLO. yeah, I think maybe it does

EVA. dance with me

CARLO. no, I should go

EVA. please
   dance with me

CARLO. one dance

        (They dance until.)

        (A send off announcement over the speakers:)

        *("The bride and groom want to thank
        everyone for making this a beautiful night.*

Let's send our newlyweds off to enjoy their happily ever after!".)

does that mean you're leaving?

EVA. yes, I have to go

CARLO.

EVA. I'm glad you came

CARLO. me too

End of Play